Stories Children Love #2

Through the Thunder-storm

by
W.G. Van de Hulst

illustrated by
Willem G. Van de Hulst, Jr.

INHERITANCE PUBLICATIONS
NEERLANDIA, ALBERTA, CANADA
PELLA, IOWA, U.S.A.

Library and Archives Canada Cataloguing in Publication
Hulst, W. G. van de (Willem Gerrit), 1879-1963
[Van Bop en Bep en Brammetje. English]
Through the thunderstorm / by W.G. Van de Hulst ; illustrated
by Willem G. Van de Hulst, Jr. ; [translated by Harry der Nederlanden].
(Stories children love ; 2)
Translation of: Van Bop en Bep en Brammetje.
Originally published: St. Catharines, Ontario : Paideia Press, 1978.
ISBN 978-1-928136-02-6 (pbk.)
I. Hulst, Willem G. van de (Willem Gerrit), 1917-, illustrator
II. Nederlanden, Harry der, translator III. Title. IV. Title: Van Bop en
Bep en Brammetje. English V. Series: Hulst, W. G. van de (Willem Gerrit),
1879-1963 Stories children love ; 2
PZ7.H873985Thro 2014   j839.313'62   C2014-903594-2

Library of Congress Cataloging-in-Publication Data
Hulst, W. G. van de (Willem Gerrit), 1879-1963.
[Van Bob en Bep en Brammetje. English.]
Through the thunderstorm / by W.G. Van de Hulst ; illustrated by Willem G. Van de Hulst,
Jr. ; edited by Paulina Janssen.
pages cm. — (Stories children love ; #2)
"Originally published in Dutch as Van Bob en Bep en Brammetje. Original translations
done by Harry der Nederlanden and Theodore Plantinga for Paideia Press, St. Catharines-
Ontario-Canada."
Summary: Bob, Betsy, and Benjamin, sent through the woods to Grandmother's house
with a basket full of strawberries, get into mischief—and have tricks played on them—
but even through a storm they are watched over by the birds and the Lord.
ISBN 978-1-928136-02-6
[1. Brothers and sisters—Fiction. 2. Behavior—Fiction. 3. Thunderstorms—Fiction.] I.
Hulst, Willem G. van de (Willem Gerrit), 1917- illustrator. II. Title.
PZ7.H887Thr 2014   [E]—dc23   2014017982

Originally published in Dutch as *Van Bob en Bep en Brammetje*
Cover painting and illustrations by Willem G. Van de Hulst, Jr.
Original translations done by Harry der Nederlanden and Theodore Plantinga
for Paideia Press, St. Catharines-Ontario-Canada.
The publisher expresses his appreciation to John Hultink of Paideia Press for
his generous permission to use his translation (ISBN 0-88815-502-6).

Edited by Paulina Janssen

ISBN 978-1-928136-02-6

Published simultaneously in U.S.A. by Inheritance Publications
Box 366, Pella, Iowa 50219

Printed in Canada

Contents

1. The Wooden Shoes

Look! Three pairs of wooden shoes. Six shoes all alone in the woods — whose were they? They must belong to three children.

Two of the shoes were very, very small.

Look! A fat little frog hopped along. With his big eyes he stared at the wooden shoes. He was a nosy frog.

He thought, "What are those things? Are they little wooden houses? I'd better take a look."

He jumped on top of one of them. Then he hopped inside. He sat still in the little, dark room.

But those three children — where were they?

Mr. Frog sat proudly looking around his little room.

It was very quiet in the woods.

2. The Fat Baker

Along came a fat baker.
His rosy red face was always smiling.
In the trees the birds were chirping.
When the baker heard their songs, he felt
happy. Then he sang a little song too.
He was carrying a huge basket on his arm.
The basket was very heavy, but he was so
happy that he did not even notice.
The sun shone brightly on that warm day.
The baker went on singing. He had rosy red
cheeks and he always smiled.
Suddenly, he stood still.
He stopped singing too.
He saw the three pairs
of wooden shoes.
Whose were they?
They must belong to
three little children.

The big, fat baker laughed. He thought, "I'll play a trick on them."
He picked up one of the wooden shoes and hung it on a branch.

The big fat baker did not see the little fat frog. Poor frightened frog! He peeked out of his dark little room.

Plop! Out he jumped, right on top of the fat baker's cap.

"Oh! What's that?" the baker cried. He jumped in fright.

The fat frog jumped too. Plop! Into the grass. Away he hopped, through the trees, toward the water. Splash! He dove in headfirst. "Was I ever scared!" he thought. "I'll never crawl into a dark room like that again. No, never!"

The big, fat baker laughed. His rosy cheeks shone merrily.

Then he walked on, singing another little song. And the birds sang with him.

3. Barefoot

Beyond the trees was a large, shallow pool of water.

Listen! The water splashed and splattered.

There they came, the three children — Bob and Betsy and Benjamin.

They were wading barefoot in the water. Splish, splash! Splish, splash!

The noise frightened the fat little frog. He ducked under a large leaf floating on the water. He thought to himself, "Go away, you little busybodies! This isn't your pond. It's ours. It's a frog pond. Go away!"

Bob and Betsy and Benjamin had been walking through the woods on an errand for their mother. They had to bring some strawberries to their grandmother — a whole basketful. Look, the basket stood on the grass.

The lid was tightly closed.

But Bob had said, "I know. Let's wade in the pond."

Betsy was a little scared.

But Benjamin wasn't.

They pulled off their wooden shoes. And then their socks.

They set their basket under the bushes.

"Come on," said Bob. "I'm not scared."

"Come on," said Benjamin. "Me not scared."

In they went, all three of them — Bob and Betsy and Benjamin.

Bob said, "Shall we catch some fish?"

"Yes!" said Betsy. "And then Grandma can cook them for us."

Benjamin said, "Me catch a great big shark."

They went far out into the water.

It wasn't deep at all.

They splashed and splooshed. But they did not see a single fish.

Suddenly, little Benjamin began to wail.

"Ow, ow! Help! Help! A big shark bit me, bit my foot!"

He lifted one foot high out of the water, crying in alarm.

Silly little Benjamin! He had stepped on a branch lying on the bottom of the pond. A twig had stabbed him between his toes.

Silly Benjamin. Bob and Betsy made fun of him.

There they came, the three of them, little Benjamin in the middle. They jumped up and down, splashing with delight.

But Benjamin kept looking at his toes. He was still worried that a shark might bite him.

Splish, splash! Splish, splash!

4. Wooden Apples

"Oh . . . What happened to my wooden shoes?" Bob cried.

"Oh! My wooden shoes are gone!" Betsy cried.

"My wooden shoes gone too!" Benjamin cried.

They looked at each other. Their cheeks turned pale with worry.

"Oh, my wooden shoes! Where have they gone?"

They looked everywhere.

Tears gathered in Betsy's eyes.

"Oh, where are my wooden shoes?"

Then, high in a tree, a finch started to whistle:

Tweedlee-tweet, tweedlee-tweet!
A little riddle for bare little feet:
There's fruit in the tree,
But it's not very sweet.
Tweedlee, tweedlee, tweedlee-tweet!

Benjamin looked up at the bird.

Oh, and then he spotted the wooden shoes

hanging in the tree. "My . . . my . . . !" he squealed.

He pulled at Betsy's skirt and at Bob's pants, and he hollered, "My . . . my . . . my . . . !"

"What is it, Benjamin? What is it?"

"My . . . my . . . I see them! There! There!"

Oh, yes, there were their wooden shoes — up in the tree.

What a relief!

Bob quickly found a big stick in the woods. He shook the branches with it.

Betsy held out her skirt to catch the wooden shoes. One of them fell down just like an apple falls from a tree.

Silly little Benjamin stood underneath with his hands spread out.

Another one fell down — right on Benjamin's nose. "Ouch!"

All the wooden shoes fell down like apples fall from a tree.

"Let's go," Bob said. "It's getting late."

They began to walk as fast as they could.

Bob and Betsy carried the basket of big, juicy strawberries for Grandma.

Benjamin skipped on ahead.

He sang, "I found the wooden shoes. I am
smart!"
Bob said, "I wonder who hid them?"
Betsy said, "I don't know . . ."

And they looked around, just a little bit
frightened, at the deep, dark woods.

High in the trees the finch sang:
  Tweedlee-tweet! Tweedlee-tweet!
  A little riddle for dry little feet:
  He makes your bread,
  And he makes it sweet.
  Tweedlee, tweedlee, tweedlee-tweet!

5. The Angry Old Woman

The children walked down a long, windy path.
They came to a wheelbarrow.
Piled on that wheelbarrow were lots and lots
of dead, dry branches.
A little old woman had gathered them in the
woods and had loaded them on her wheel-
barrow. She was happy. Now she could go
home and start a fire.
Then she could cook her supper — potatoes
with bacon. And a few green peas from her
garden.
She was pleased with her big load of wood.
She now only needed a few small, dry twigs.
She walked back into the bushes to find them.
She wore dark glasses because the sun hurt
her eyes.
And her back ached from bending over.
But she was happy all the same.

Oh, no!
Bob tugged at her wood.
He had not seen the old woman; he only saw
the wheelbarrow.

He pulled at a branch but the branch was stuck.

The pile swayed.

Bob tugged harder.

Betsy came to help.

And Benjamin said, "I can pull too. I'm strong."

Look out!

Suddenly, the whole wheelbarrow tipped over.

The wood scattered across the grass.

Bob and Betsy and Benjamin stood still, staring in fright.

Then they ran away as fast as they could.

The basket full of strawberries bounced along with them.

Just then the old woman came from behind the bushes. She had seen the accident.

"Oh, you little rascals!" she cried. "Now I
have to pick it all up again. And I'm so tired.
And my back is so sore! Just watch out! If I
ever get my hands on you . . . !"
She shook her fist in the air and scowled
angrily through her dark glasses.
She was not very happy anymore.

For a moment, Bob looked back. Betsy and Benjamin looked back too.

Bob said, "Never mind. Come on! She can't catch us anyway."

"She's a wicked witch!" Betsy cried. "If she catches us, she'll eat us all up."

And Benjamin yelled, "I'm scared! She eat me up!" He held on to Betsy's skirt and tried very hard to keep up with his chubby little legs.

He walked so fast that the tip of his tongue peeked out of the corner of his mouth.

Suddenly, Bob said, "I've got it! That old woman is probably the one who hid our wooden shoes. I'm sure she did it!"

"Yes! For sure!" Betsy said.

"Wicked woman!" Benjamin mumbled.

The poor old woman had to pick up all the branches again.

No, she was not very happy anymore.

She was so old!

She was so tired!

And her back was so sore!

Poor woman!

6. Grandma's House

There was Grandma's house.
Grandma was standing in the doorway.
"Hello, Grandma! How are you?"
"Hello, children. What a surprise! Did you come through the woods all by yourselves? Come right inside Grandma's house. My, my! And you brought Grandma something? Wasn't that sweet of you! Come on. Come right in. My, my! And is all of it for Grandma?
"Oh, dear. Look at that! They're all smashed. You must have shaken them too much. It looks like strawberry soup!
"But that's all right. We'll pick out the ones that aren't smashed and we'll eat the others right away. All right? I'll put a little sugar on them. Strawberry soup with sugar! Won't that taste good?"
Quickly the children sat around the table.

They each got a dishful of strawberries — smashed strawberries sprinkled with sugar! Delicious!

Then they went outside to play with Grandma's white goat.

When the goat jumped he looked so funny, and he made such silly sounds. Ba-a-a-a!

Then Grandma made pancakes. They smelled delicious and they tasted even better. Finally Grandma said, "It is time to hurry home, children. Just look at that sky! Do you see those clouds over there? We may be in for a thunderstorm. Go straight home and don't stop to play. If you get caught in a thunderstorm . . ."

They all gave Grandma a big hug and showered her with kisses.

"My, my!" Grandma laughed, gasping for air. "What roughnecks you are!"

Off they ran.

Benjamin hollered, "I run fast, really fast."

Thump! There he went — flat on his face!

He hurt his knee, but he still laughed a little. Then he limped along behind Bob and Betsy as fast as he could.

Grandma smiled and waved. "Be careful! And

keep going. Don't stop to play. Don't stop
for anything. Go straight home. Look at that
sky!"

Grandma waved again and watched from the
doorway until the three children were out of
sight.

Then she went inside.

She sighed, "I hope they keep right on going.
They have to get home before that thunderstorm . . ."

7. Poor Little Bird

Somewhere in the woods stood a big tree.
In the tree was a big, black hole.
At the foot of the tree sat a finch.
Bob saw it.
Whoosh! His wooden shoe flew through the air.
Oh! It almost hit the little bird.
Terribly frightened, the bird flit right into the big, black hole in the tree.
And then?
Bob snuck up to the tree. Suddenly, he clamped his wooden shoe over the hole.
Then the frightened little bird could not get out.
It was trapped.

"There, there," Bob said.

Slowly he put his hand into the hole. The little bird chirped in fear.

But Bob grabbed it anyway.

And Benjamin said, "A birdy, a birdy! I catch a birdy too!"

"Let me see!" Betsy said.

"Me too! Me see it too!"

Bob held the little bird cupped between his hands. Frightened, it twittered unhappily.

"Poor little bird," Betsy said. "Let it go. It looks so frightened!"

"No! Why should I?" Bob snapped.

Benjamin begged, "Me hold the birdy too? Me hold it too?"

"No! You're too small."

Then Bob had an idea.

"I know!" he said. "I know! We'll put the bird in the basket. All right? It's empty anyway."

"Yes! Yes! In the basket!" Benjamin cried.

He lifted the lid off the basket.

"No, no. Just open it a little way," Bob snapped. Then . . . plop! Into the basket went the little bird and the lid slammed shut.

The three children danced around the basket in delight.

"We caught a bird! We caught a bird!"

The poor little bird fluttered around in the empty basket, terribly upset and frightened.

"Listen," Bob said. "We'll go find some worms for the little bird — a big bunch of worms. All right? Then we'll put them in the basket. Otherwise the bird will starve to death. The little bird will like worms. Are you coming?"

"Yes, yes! Me too! Me too!" Benjamin said.

"No, not you. You have to look after the basket."

"Me? All right," Benjamin said.

Thump! he sat down — right on the basket. Then the bird could not get away.

Bob and Betsy went off into the bushes. They pulled up clumps of grass to find worms. Slowly they wandered farther and farther away . . .

The sky was getting darker and darker, but they did not notice.

Grandma had told them, "Go straight home."

But they had forgotten her warning.
Benjamin got tired of waiting.
He said, "I can look for worms too!"
But what about the basket?
Benjamin knew what to do.

He put the basket down right by the big black
hole in the hollow tree.
Off he ran.

And the basket stayed behind, all alone.

8. Another Trick

Along came the big fat baker again.
He had rosy red cheeks and he smiled.
He was singing a song just like the birds in
the trees.
It was very warm in the woods and he was
carrying a heavy basket.
But he was too happy to feel hot and tired.
Suddenly, he stood still.
He stopped singing too.
He saw something next to the hollow tree.
And he heard something.
What could that be?
He bent down to listen. What could that be?
He pulled the basket toward him and listened
again, first with one ear, then with the other.
Then he laughed.
"So! Now I've got it. It's a little bird — a
poor, trapped little bird. Let me see . . ."
He peered through a little crack in the lid.
"Poor little bird! So unhappy!
"You sound so scared! You poor thing!
"You don't belong in a basket. You belong
up in the trees, up in the wide, blue sky.

"You shouldn't be making those unhappy sounds. You should be singing pretty songs. But you can't do that in a basket.

"Did those foolish little children put you in there? That wasn't very kind, was it? Or very smart!

"Come on, you poor little thing. Out of that basket. Fly away and join the other little birds in the woods. Go and sing your songs again — your nice, happy songs."

The baker threw the lid of the basket open.

"Tweedlee-tweet!" chirped the little bird and away it flew. It flew high up into the trees and hid itself among the leaves. "Tweedlee-tweet!"

The big fat baker laughed at the little bird.

And then . . .

Then he took three things out of his own basket and put them in the children's basket. He laughed again.

He put the basket with the three things in it back by the hollow tree, with the lid closed, just as he had found it.

Then he hurried off.

"Foolish little rascals," he chuckled. "I tricked you again. Ha-ha-ha!"

High up in the top of the tallest tree the happy bird sang its merry song:

Tweedlee-tweet! Tweedlee-tweet!
I was so scared, they had me beat.
But open the lid and you will see
A ransom which is very sweet.
Tweedlee, tweedlee, tweedlee-tweet!

9. The Thunderstorm

Bob and Betsy and Benjamin were still looking for worms.
They had not found a single one.
Benjamin saw a couple of acorns.
He quickly put them in his pocket and said, "I'll give acorns to birdy."
"Silly! Birds don't like acorns."
"I'll give them anyway."
The sky was getting darker and darker.
The wind rushed wildly through the trees. The trees rustled restlessly.
The dark sky began to rumble.

Suddenly, the children were frightened.
They forget all about the worms and the acorns.
They remembered Grandma's warning, "We may be in for a thunderstorm. Don't stop to play."
The rumbling in the dark sky put terror in their hearts.
Betsy pulled at Bob's shirt.
"Come on, Bob. Let's go home. Quick! I'm getting scared!"

Benjamin hid his face in Betsy's skirt and cried, "Me scared! Me scared!"

And Bob, the oldest, said, "Let's go, then. Hurry up!"

Off they ran — through the bushes, to the long winding path.

Benjamin ran between Bob and Betsy. They held on to him tightly.

"Come on! Come on! Hurry!"

Benjamin lost one of his wooden shoes. "Oooh! My wooden shoe!"

Betsy tore her skirt on a branch. "Oooh! My skirt, my skirt!"

And Bob cut his hand on a thorny bush. "Ouch! Ouch!"

The dark sky grumbled and rumbled.

Splat! Splat! Splatter-splat! It starting raining.

Splat! Splatter-splatter, splat-splat!

The raindrops were huge.

They splattered on the leaves of the trees. They splattered on the path. And they splattered on Benjamin's nose when he looked up. Splat! Splat! Splatter-splat!

It started to rain hard.

"The basket! The basket!" Bob cried.

He snatched it away from the hollow tree and ran on.

The little bird? Everyone had forgotten him.

When the lightning flashed it seemed as if the whole woods was filled with fire.

A terrible thunderclap rolled through the sky. The earth trembled as if the trees were tumbling over one another. The sky rumbled and rumbled.

"Mother, Mother! I'm scared!" Benjamin wailed.

Betsy also began to cry. "Mother! Mother! Oh, Mother, help!"

And Bob shivered with fear. He thought of Mother too. She would probably be very angry with them. But — Mother was so far away!

"A house! A house! I see a house!" Bob shouted.

They ran to the house as fast as they could. A large wheelbarrow stood in front of the door.

A lot of dead branches were piled on the wheelbarrow.

The door opened slowly. Someone came outside. What a terrible fright they got then! It was the old woman with the dark glasses! The children — oh, they wanted to fly far away.

But they were too scared to move.

They thought, "That old woman is very angry at us because we tipped over her wheelbarrow."

But the old woman said, "You poor lambs. Quick! Come inside!"

She took Benjamin into her arms and quickly carried him into the house.

"Me scared! She eat me up!" he wailed.
Bob and Betsy followed. What else could they do? But they trembled with fear.
"Put the basket down in the corner," the old woman said.

Outside, the thunder rumbled on.
The rain splattered against the small windows of the cottage.
The wind whipped wildly and the little cottage shook.
The poor trees groaned.

10. Close Together

"No, no! I go to Mother," Benjamin cried, struggling to get loose.
Then the old woman said, "Don't be afraid, little boy. I'm not angry anymore."
But Benjamin cried, "She eat me up!"
The old woman could not help but laugh.
"Now I understand. You are afraid of these dark glasses, aren't you? Children are always afraid of them. Calm down. I'll take these ugly glasses off. There! Is that better?"

Then the children saw that the old woman really had very friendly eyes.

No, now she did not look scary at all.

She looked just as friendly as Grandma.

Then they were not afraid of her anymore.

Not even Benjamin.

When the thunder rumbled, he crawled right up against her, pressing his face against her cheek. Betsy sat on a footstool close to her. She snuggled up to the old woman.

When the lightning flashed and the thunder rumbled, Betsy put her face in the old woman's lap.

And Bob?

He stood close by the arm of her chair.

The old woman put her arm around him, just as a grandmother would do.

"Calm down, calm down, children," she said. "Don't be afraid. Just stay close to me. Don't be afraid."

They sat together as closely as possible.

And Bob thought to himself, "I'll never tip her wheelbarrow over again. Never!"

11. Very Quietly!

Their fear of the old woman was gone, but not their fear of the thunder.

The rain clattered down on the roof.

Every now and then, a terribly bright light flashed through the room — lightning!

Even when they closed their eyes tightly, they could still see the terrible light.

Then, suddenly, the rumbling began again. Horrible! It sounded as if the whole sky was about to fall down on them.

They trembled.

But the old woman was not afraid at all.

She held her arms around the three children. She closed her friendly eyes. She prayed without speaking. When the thunder passed, it was very, very quiet in the room.

The old woman finally said, "I have asked the Lord to watch over us. The thunderstorm won't be able to hurt us because the Lord will take care of us. He sees us in the thunderstorm here in the middle of the woods. He sees us all the time."

Bob thought, "The Lord sees us always. He

also saw that we stopped to play in the woods after Grandma told us not to. And He also saw us put that poor little bird in our basket. And I'm the oldest. It's all my fault."
Quietly Bob closed his eyes and prayed. No one saw it. No one could hear what he said. But the Lord saw and heard.
The Lord saw everything and He heard everything.

Bob looked at the basket standing in a dark corner by the door.
He listened. Nothing.
He wondered, "Could the bird be sleeping?"
Then he thought, "Could the bird be dead?"
He turned pale at the thought.

12. Who Did It?

The thunderstorm lasted a long time, but finally it blew over.
"Well, children, time to hurry home," the old woman said.
She took a little jar from her cupboard.

Benjamin watched eagerly.

She popped a big round candy into the mouth of each child.

"Good-bye, children! Good-bye!"

Away they went.

Benjamin walked in the middle and Bob carried the basket.

They walked along quickly.

The air was nice and cool out in the woods after the storm.

The sun broke through the clouds.

On the trees millions of water droplets hung, like tiny silver beads.

Plink! Plink! Plinketty-plink! they fell.

Plink! Plinketty-plink! Plinketty-plink!

The silver beads fell one by one on the basket. And when Benjamin looked up they fell on his nose.

Plink! Plink! Plinketty-plink!

The children were not afraid anymore. They laughed at all those silver beads.

Benjamin looked up again.

He said, "Look! Me not scared. Fall, little drops. Fall on Benjamin's nose."

Ptooie! One of the drops fell right into his open mouth.
Ptooie!

They reached the long winding path.
Suddenly, Bob said, "Listen! Shall we let the little bird go?"
"Yes," Betsy said. "That's a good idea!"
And Benjamin said, "Me too! Me too!"
Bob put the basket down on the ground.
All three of them knelt in a circle around the basket.
"Shhh! I don't hear anything."
Bob listened with his ear on the lid of the basket.
"Oh, no! What if the little bird is dead?" Betsy asked.
Bob turned pale again, thinking, "It's my fault."
"Me look! Me look!" cried Benjamin.

Bob opened the basket just a tiny crack.
"Careful, now," said Betsy.
All three of them peered in through the crack.
They saw nothing.

They heard nothing.
They opened the basket a little further.
But there was no bird that flew out.
Then . . . they opened the basket wide.
And then there was still no bird that flew out.

But . . . !
"Oh!" they all cried at the same time.
"Oh, look!"
"Look! Look!"

There, on the bottom, lay three raisin buns.

"Oh, look, oh, look!"

Who put them there?

Bob did not know.

Betsy did not know.

And Benjamin did not know at all.

They chattered happily.

Who hung their wooden shoes up in the tree?
Not the old woman. She wasn't a wicked
woman. She was a good woman.

Who put the raisin buns in their basket?
Not the old woman. No one touched the
basket after it was put in the corner.

But who then? Who?

"Me taste one," Benjamin said.

"No, you don't," Bob said. "We're going to
tell Mother first."

"Yes, that's right!" cried Betsy.

"Yes, right!" cried Benjamin. "Me too!"

Off they dashed — straight for home.
The three raisin buns bounced around in the
empty basket.
"Oh, I wonder who did it!"
High among the dripping leaves, the little
finch sang his song:

Tweedlee-tweet! Tweedlee-tweet!
Who played a trick on wet little feet?
Who let the little bird fly?
And who put in a treat?
Tweedlee, tweedlee, tweedlee-tweet!

13. Good Night!

It was night.
The moon peeked from behind the chimney.
Stars twinkled in the sky.
Look! At the door stood the wooden shoes
— all alone.
Whose were they?
They belonged to three little children.
And where were those children now?
They were fast asleep, tucked in their beds.

They had told the whole story to their mother.
Mother had been worried and a little angry.
But not for long.

Mother had asked, "Were you very scared out in the woods?"
Benjamin said, "The Lord take care of me."
Mother let them eat their raisin buns before they said their evening prayers.
Then — under the covers they went.

It was nighttime.
The moon peeked from behind the chimney.
Stars twinkled in the sky.
Look! At the door stood the wooden shoes — all alone.

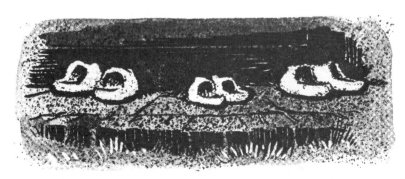

Titles in this series: